Alina in the Deep

Praise for *Alina in a Pinch*

★ Forest of Reading Silver Birch Express Award Finalist
★ The Hackmatack Children's Choice Book Award Finalist

"Alina's relationship with Nani is heartfelt, and the protagonist's growing self-assuredness and perseverance will be a comfort for fellow new kids who see themselves in her struggles."

—*Publishers Weekly*

"A smart, timely tale of acceptance, pride, and identity, *Alina in a Pinch* is a book that has you cheering for its plucky protagonist."

—*Open Book*

"This is more than a story about fitting in. Alina realizes that her classmates also have insecurities and differences and comes to accept her background. She looks forward to celebrating it as she tries for a title of Junior Chef."

—Helen Norrie, *Winnipeg Free Press*

"This chapter book will guide readers into diversity and equity and acceptance…and not just because of the food we eat."

—Larry Swartz, *Dr. Larry Recommends*

"I think kids should read this book because it's very informative about culture and that you should express it if you enjoy it. You should not hide what you like just because other people don't agree with it."

—*EMWF Children's Book Reviews*

ALINA IN THE DEEP

Shenaaz Nanji

Second Story Press

Library and Archives Canada Cataloguing in Publication

Title: Alina in the deep / Shenaaz Nanji.
Names: Nanji, Shenaaz, author.
Description: Series statement: Alina ; 2
Identifiers: Canadiana (print) 20240339053 | Canadiana (ebook) 20240339061 | ISBN 9781772603903 (softcover) | ISBN 9781772604009 (EPUB)
Subjects: LCGFT: Novels.
Classification: LCC PS8577.A573 A78 2024 | DDC jC813/.54—dc23

Copyright © 2024 by Shenaaz Nanji
Cover and illustrations by Beena Mistry
Printed and bound in Canada

Second Story Press gratefully acknowledges the support of the Ontario Arts Council and the Canada Council for the Arts for our publishing program. We acknowledge the financial support of the Government of Canada through the Canada Book Fund.

Second Story Press expressly prohibits the use of *Alina in the Deep* in connection with the development of any software program, including, without limitation, training a machine learning or generative artificial intelligence (AI) system.

Published by
SECOND STORY PRESS
20 Maud Street, Suite 401
Toronto, ON M5V 2M5
www.secondstorypress.ca

With love to Lux and Liam.

Always march to the beat of your own drum.

Chapter 1
CLOUD NINE

Alina was floating on cloud nine. She broke into a dance in her room, her blue hoodie flying as she sang ever so loudly to her pet dog, Lux.

"Whoa-whoa-whoa, summer of a lifetime!"

Lux rolled over to show his belly, whining.

Alina went down on her knees. "Here," she said, giving Lux a good belly rub. "Don't get your furry self into knots. I won't leave you. My first love, right? Joined at the hip." She cuddled him and he nose-bumped her.

Alina had everything she wanted. Well, everything except a sibling. And sometimes being an only child got lonely, especially during holidays.

With siblings, you're never alone, she thought. Her best friends, Kim and Liam, had siblings. Ready-made friends. It must be like having sleepovers every day.

Lux climbed into Alina's lap and lay like a furry ball. She stroked him. Siblings have your back. When Kim was upset, she'd run to her brother and Liam to his sister. Alina wished for that too. What adventures they'd have. They'd share silly jokes and secrets. Things she couldn't tell her parents.

Now her dream of having a sibling would come true. In 120 minutes…um…7,200 seconds, her cousin Safi from Kenya would land at the Calgary airport.

"Lux, up, up." Alina rose to her feet. "There." She found some chalk and wrote on the board her dream list of fun things to do this summer with her cousin.

1. **Wear hoodies and hang around like twinsies.**
2. **Binge-watch TV.**

3. Hike, bike, have fun with Lux.
4. Go wild and crazy—dye their hair blue.
5. Soccer camp. Yippee!
6. Go to the Stampede as cowgirls. Yahoo!
7. Mess around with new recipes for her *Yummy Tummy* food show and get a zillion followers.
8. Water balloon fights!!!

Yippee! Alina leaped and cartwheeled across her room, her blue hoodie flying.

She began to sing to herself. No school, no homework, no tests.

She could not wait to spend the lazy, crazy summer with her cousin, Safi, and Lux.

Chapter 2

CALGARY AIRPORT

Sometimes, time gets stuck, thought Alina. She was at the arrivals area in the Calgary airport with Lux and her parents. They were waiting for Safi to arrive, but the flight was delayed. It was hard to just stand there and wait. And wait and *wait*.

"C'mon, let's explore." Alina led Lux, weaving her way through everyone waiting to welcome their loved ones.

There were gorillas, Indigenous teepees, and works of art on display by the Calgary Zoo. Last year, her parents went to Kenya to help take care of Safi's mother, Alina's Aunt Guli. She had sadly died after a long sickness.

Alina stopped to show Lux the huge, sculpted dinosaur chomping suitcases when she caught sight of a tall girl in a red and green salwar kameez. The girl was exiting from the gate, sashaying her way in a pair of golden sandals.

Alina's heart skipped a few beats. She stopped mid-stride. It was her.

Safi's Indian outfit with *zari*-threaded flowers sparkled, and the gold in her ears, neck, and arms flashed brightly.

Alina's stomach sank. Yes, Alina had a few lehengas and salwar kameez outfits. They made her feel like a queen, but she only wore them on special occasions. Like festivals and weddings. Mostly, she wore leggings like her friends did. She didn't like to stand out, it attracted attention. Also, it made belonging hard. It had taken a long time for her to fit in at her new school. It was only after the incident with the lunch bully that she got accepted. She didn't want to ruin all that.

"C'mon, Lux." She made her way back through the crowd. Last year, she had struggled to combine

her two cultures. Sometimes she was afraid of being too Indian for her classmates and sometimes she was afraid of being too western for her Indian friends and family. It was a delicate balance.

Safi was Kenyan, of course. Alina hadn't realized how much Safi would stand out.

Alina joined her parents, glancing nervously at the people around her. She didn't see any familiar faces.

"There she is. Safi, Safi!" Mom cried.

Alina caught a lady staring at them. She pulled her hoodie over her head and looked down.

"Aunty, Uncle," cried Safi, walking with open arms.

Lux growled. "She's a friend," said Alina, pulling at his leash. She looked up and Safi smiled shyly, her skin glowing like a model in a magazine.

Her parents embraced Safi. "*Karibu*, welcome," said Mom in Swahili, one of the languages spoken in Kenya. Tears ran down Dad's face. Alina had never seen Dad cry.

The girls hugged each other briefly.

"Welcome to Calgary, one of the best cities in the world," said Alina.

Safi smiled a half smile, her eyes lined thickly in dark kohl.

Salty greeting, thought Alina.

"Woof, woof," Lux barked. Lux didn't like strangers.

"Hello, cutie." Safi bent to pat Lux, and he wagged his tail. "I'll get my bags," said Safi in a thick accent.

Alina's dad put his arm around Safi as they made their way to the baggage carousel. *Tup, tup, tup*, Safi took dainty little steps, her earrings and braid swinging.

Alina's breath whooshed through her pursed lips, her stomach sinking further. Her cousin looked so glamorous. Alina always dressed plain. Basic. Her friends called her a hoodie girl. How could they be twinsies? They looked like total opposites.

Her dream list of fun things to do this summer with her cousin fizzled right out.

Chapter 3
PERSONALITY GAME

Finally, they left the airport. Alina breathed a sigh of relief. She walked ahead with Dad to the car as he pushed the luggage cart loaded with Safi's bags. Mom and Safi trailed behind.

"Dad," whispered Alina. "Safi has a strong accent." *What if people don't understand her?*

"Yes, it tells the story of who she is and her heritage. It's her badge of honor and pride."

Alina nodded, though she wasn't sure she understood.

"Sunsets during summer are late," Mom was telling Safi. It was 9 p.m. and still quite bright outside.

They got in the car. Alina sat next to her cousin in the back seat with Lux on her lap. She stroked his furry body, feeling better. Lux always calmed her down.

Mom asked Safi how her dad and her older brothers were.

"They're well, Aunty," said Safi.

Dad asked her about the pothole on the road where his car had gotten stuck last year.

Safi laughed. "Uncle, it's bigger, deeper, and muddier. We can swim in it." She said the long rains had washed out many roads.

Alina waited for the road talk to end but Safi looked out the car window. "The road here is so wide and smooth and squeaky clean. Are all of them like that?"

"Yes, people have to pay fines for littering," said Dad. "In fact, the Trans-Canada Highway runs all the way from the Pacific shore in the west to the Atlantic in the east. Almost five thousand miles."

"Wow," said Safi. "It would be fun to drive across Canada."

Boring, Alina thought. She was curious to know more about Safi. She'd played the personality game with newbies at school to get to know them better. Maybe that would help. She turned to Safi. "Want to play a fun game?"

"Not now, Alee," said Mom. "Safi must be exhausted."

"Her journey was more than thirty hours," said Dad.

"I'm fine, Uncle, Aunty," said Safi sweetly.

"Okay," said Alina. "First question: Are you a dog person or cat person?"

Safi patted Lux. "I like dogs, but I guess I'm more of a *Kasuku* girl."

"What in the world is that?" asked Alina.

"Parrot," said Mom and Dad together. "Swahili for parrot."

"My uncle has one called Chatty," said Safi. "Talks nonstop. Has us all wrapped around his tail. He sings, whistles, and dances. Even smells the gummy bears hidden in my pocket."

"Really?" said Alina.

"Yes, he sits on my shoulder, nips my neck, and screeches, 'I love you,' again and again 'til I share the gummies with him."

They all laughed.

Alina patted Lux. Chatty sounded cute, but she liked Lux. "Okay, next question. Vanilla or chocolate?"

"Actually, mango," said Safi.

Alina frowned. Why didn't she pick from the choices given? "Okay, what sports do you like? Soccer or baseball?"

"I like soccer," Safi said, shrugging, "but I prefer Scrabble."

Alina frowned again. "That's a board game, not a sport." She'd try something simple. "Town girl or city girl?"

"Village girl," said Safi.

Alina gave a *Why did you come here?* look. Calgary was a city.

"Village life is filled with adventures," said Safi. "Every holiday I visit my dadi, my grandma from Dad's side. She lives in a village near Limuru. I get to milk the cows and then drink it. I get to pick and eat fresh eggs, veggies, and fruits. I even draw water from the well. You never run out of things to do. People pop in all the time."

"Nice," said Alina. Village life sounded fun. Safi was lucky. Alina wanted to visit Safi's grandmother's village.

★★★

Back home, Safi politely declined to eat. She wanted to go to sleep. Alina helped carry Safi's bag upstairs to the guest room. It was right next to her bedroom.

"This one's mine. C'mon in," said Alina, showing off her normally wrecked room. She had cleaned up to impress her cousin.

Safi scanned Alina's room, her eyes getting bigger every second. The green rug looked like grass, and the top part of the blue walls and ceiling were painted with fluffy white clouds. Just like the sky. Her room was styled to look like a soccer field.

"Wow!" said Safi.

"Credit to good old Dad," said Alina.

"My mom's also artistic...." Safi went quiet. "I mean, she was."

Alina's stomach plummeted. She couldn't imagine what it was like to lose a parent. Then the phone rang, and she couldn't help feeling relieved. It saved her from having to find something to say.

It was Nani from Edmonton, Alina's M.F.P., or Most Favorite Person. Safi talked to Nani first, and Nani welcomed Safi. Then Safi handed the phone back to Alina, whispered goodnight, and left.

"I miss you," Alina told Nani when she was alone. She and Nani were like two halves of a whole. "When are you coming?"

"After your sports camp, *beta*," said Nani. "I'm so glad Safi's here. You'll have fun together."

Alina lowered her voice. "Nani, she's a bit weird."

"In what way?" asked Nani.

"She doesn't look or speak like anyone in my class," said Alina. "How will she blend in with my friends?"

"Alee, Alee, we too were immigrants," said Nani. "I still feel like I have one foot in Kenya, the other in Canada."

"Oh," said Alina.

"In fact, your parents and I must have looked very different from what people were used to when we first came to Canada." Nani chuckled.

"Right," said Alina. She had totally forgotten that.

"Give her time, Alee. Little by little the bird makes its nest, *na*? You will have so much fun together."

"Yes," said Alina, but she wasn't too sure. Safi was a lot different than what she had expected.

Chapter 4

WHAT A LETDOWN

"Okay, Luxster. Walkie time," said Alina. She and Dad had a ritual—every Sunday before breakfast they raced along with Lux at the Glenmore Reservoir.

Lux wagged his tail and stood upright to lick her face.

Alina led Lux downstairs to the family room. Her dad was still reading the newspaper. "C'mon Dad," she said. "Five-dollar fine for being late."

"Shhh," said Mom. "Safi's asleep."

Dad's reading glasses slid down his nose as he looked up. "Sweetie, got to axe the walk today," he said softly.

Alina's shoulders slouched. "Why?"

"It's Safi's first day," said Dad. "I'd like to be here when she wakes up."

Alina shrugged. *But Mom was home. Why are they making Safi's arrival such a big deal?* She pulled at Lux's leash and left, letting the door bang behind her.

★★★

Back home after the walk, Alina took in the delicious smell wafting from the kitchen. A stack of freshly fried golden parathas rested on the table.

"Yum, Aloo Paratha," said Alina. The flatbread stuffed with spicy potatoes was her favorite snack. "I'm starving." She pulled out the chair and sat, waiting for her parents to join her.

But they remained seated on the couch.

"Don't tell me you guys are waiting for Safi?" said Alina.

Dad and Mom exchanged an uneasy glance.

"Your call," said Alina. She raised her fork. "For all you know it could be noon by the time she finally gets up," she said and began to eat to her heart's content.

"Mmm…crispy and flaky," she said. "These are perfect, Mom."

"Thanks," said Mom, sitting next to her. "Do you know our culture regards guests as gods?"

"Oh," said Alina. She realized with a pang that her mom had cooked the paratha for their godly guest, not for her.

"Woof, woof!" Lux barked to signal the new visitor.

Tup, tup, tup. Safi came down the stairs in her Indian *chappals*, sandals. Lux ran to sniff her.

"Hello cutie," said Safi. She looked at Alina's parents. "I'm *so* sorry Aunty and Uncle, I overslept. My day and night have flipped."

They joined Alina at the table.

"Aunty, the paratha is so good," said Safi sweetly.

They talked about the amazing fruits they had eaten in Nairobi: passion fruit, *sitaphal*, or custard apple, guavas, durian.

Alina had never been to Kenya. The strange fruits meant nothing to her. She waited for them to finish.

Then they began to talk about their incredible safari trip to Masai Mara. They had come upon a family of lions feasting on a dead animal just fifteen feet away from their car. They'd seen a blind rhino at the animal orphanage and baby elephants rolling around in a mud bath.

Alina felt a twinge of envy. Her favorite animal was the elephant. How amazing would it be to see wild animals roam freely instead of being caged at the zoo.

"The most memorable of all was the Great Migration," said Mom. "What a miracle seeing thousands of wildebeest and zebras trot across the Savannah grass. They were looking for water and better pasture," she explained to Alina.

Alina had seen the movie *The Lion King* and felt jealous. If only she had been there. She bit the string of her hoodie.

It wasn't fair. They were talking about all the interesting things they had seen without her. She had missed it all.

Dad recalled the "beast of a feast" at a Nairobi restaurant. "Imagine," he eyed Alina, "they carved the meat right onto our plates with Masai swords."

Mom squealed, giggling.

Alina had nothing to add to their adventures. She dragged her chair against the tile floor letting it screech, a cue that she was about to get up.

But she didn't leave. That would be downright rude.

She could not understand why her cousin's arrival was making her feel so out of sorts. She had bragged about her cousin to all her friends. Now that oomph was gone. *Poof.*

She closed her eyes momentarily, feeling swamped by too many emotions. It was like she was at the bottom of the sea, and she felt like she was drowning.

Chapter 5

OUTSIDER

In the afternoon, Dad took them all for a drive to show Safi downtown Calgary and other cool parts of the city.

Alina found it rather boring in the car as they passed the Calgary Tower, the City Hall, and the Olympic Plaza.

It was much better when they got out and walked around the new Central Library. They stopped at a restaurant for burgers and ice cream, then drove around the Saddledome arena. It was a huge building shaped like a real horse saddle where the Calgary Flames hockey team played.

Back home, Alina stayed in her room with Lux listening to her playlist, hoping Safi would join her.

She did not. She seemed more interested in her parents.

Alina could hear the chit-chat below. Safi was talking about how sad her dad and brothers felt at the loss of their mother. Then Mom called for her. Alina rose with a sigh. "Down Lux. Got to join the fam."

She sat with Lux in the furthest corner of the family room.

"Alee, see what Safi brought." Mom unfolded the African fabric in her hands. "It's a *khanga*."

Alina frowned. The cloth was as bright and flashy as Safi. Alina much preferred muted pastel colors. Her friends often teased her for liking "old person colors."

Mom read the Swahili saying on the fabric. "What does it mean?" She looked at Safi.

Safi beamed like the noon sun. "It says when trouble comes, it's your family that supports you. Thank you for coming all the way to Kenya," she said with a smile, her dimples bigger than dimes.

Alina wished she had dimples.

Safi turned to Alina and gave her a small gift box. "A bit of Africa for you."

"Thanks," said Alina. She opened it to find a shell necklace. It was pretty, but chunky jewelry was not her style. She didn't know what to say.

"I'm told it's magical," said Safi. "May your dreams come true."

"Thanks," said Alina again. But in her mind, her summer dream had shattered like broken glass.

"It will go with any outfit," said Mom.

"Long ago, cowrie shells were used as currency," said Dad.

Alina nodded politely.

Then they talked about the drought in Kenya and how hard it was to buy enough water at the stores. How water and electricity were controlled so they didn't run out.

Once again, Alina felt left out. Like she was at a noisy party, and nobody wanted to talk to her. Her family had totally forgotten her. She rose and plopped on the sofa next to her dad.

Dad put his arm around her. "Alee, see this magnificent carving from Africa?" He ran his hands over a tall, black sculpture by his feet.

"Strange," said Alina.

"It's the Tree of Life," said Dad, glowing with pride. "Imagine, the Makonde tribe of Africa carved this from a single piece of wood."

"I see men standing on each other's heads," said Alina.

"That shows unity," said Mom. "That we are all one."

"Hmm," said Alina. *But right now, I don't feel like one of you.* She felt like a stranger in her own house. A fish-out-of-water. She picked at her skin, over an old bruise on her forearm until it turned red and hurt.

Alina had a sudden urge to leave. But where could she go?

After their phone call, Alina knew not even her nani would understand her.

Once again, the vision of struggling in the deep sea flashed in her mind. She felt like she was paddling furiously to get to the shore, but it didn't seem to be getting any closer.

Chapter 6

POLAR BEARS AND PENGUINS

The next day, Alina waited in her room until her parents had left for work. She would not wait for their godly guest to wake up. She made scrambled eggs and oatmeal for breakfast and ate by herself.

"C'mon Lux, walkie time," she said, and left.

Upon their return, Safi called Lux, but he growled. Alina saw the table was clean, the dishes washed and put away. "You didn't have to clean," she said. "We have the dishwasher."

"I'm used to cleaning up," said Safi, shrugging. She bent down to stroke Lux. "Did you have a good walk? Look, Lux is my friend."

Lux was licking her hand.

Alina sank on the sofa thinking what on her dream list of fun things they could do. Stampede was next week, then sports camp. The Stampede was a huge summer festival with games and a rodeo and so much good food. Alina couldn't wait. But that was still days away. What could they do today? Ah, they could binge-watch TV!

"Let's watch *The Little Mermaid*," Alina said. "I've watched it a hundred times. I never get tired of it."

Safi just made a face.

"What about *The Lion King*?" asked Alina.

Safi giggled. "I come from the land of the lions," she said. "I've watched that movie so many times, I know the dialogue by heart."

"Okay, how about *Frozen*?" said Alina.

"I'm too old for all those movies," said Safi. "Can we watch an old Hindi movie? They're so emotional and romantic."

"No," said Alina firmly. Old movies were for old people. Besides, she didn't understand Hindi anyway. TV would not work. She crossed it off her list in her head.

~~2. Binge-watch TV.~~

What else could they do? Too bad the *Junior Chef* contest show wasn't in the summer.

"Let's do something radical," said Alina.

"Like what?" said Safi, kneading her hands together.

"Dye our hair blue?" said Alina.

Safi shrugged. "Aunty won't like that," she said.

Alina swallowed, disappointed. She crossed off another fun item from her list in her head.

~~4. Go wild and crazy—dye their hair blue.~~

They sat and played with Lux.

"I've an idea," said Safi suddenly. "Do you have henna?"

Alina nodded. "Mom uses it in her hair," she said.

"I can paint a henna tattoo for you," said Safi.

"Can you really?" said Alina, jumping to her feet, different designs already flashing through her mind. "Great! Let's do it."

They went to the kitchen. Alina found the henna powder and put it in a bowl.

Safi added some lemon juice and warm water to the henna powder and mixed it into a paste. She sat on the floor and spread an old towel on her lap. Then she held up a toothpick. "I'm ready," she said.

"I'm not," said Alina. "I can't decide on the tattoo. Do I go for the Alberta Wild Rose or the peace sign, or…. Oh, I know, I want a dainty little butterfly. Can you do that?"

"Sure," said Safi.

Alina sat on the kitchen floor and let her hand rest on the towel in Safi's lap. Safi dipped the toothpick in the henna paste and began to paint it, dot by dot, on Alina's palm.

"May I ask why a butterfly?" said Safi.

"'Cause my Nani always says, 'Alee, stop being a caterpillar.' She means that sometimes it's helpful to like, let go of the old and welcome in the new. Break out of my comfy cocoon and morph into a butterfly."

"That's me too," said Safi, looking up at Alina. "I'm stuck in my cocoon. I still carry my mom here." She put her hand over her heart. "I feel I cannot go on without her. I know it will pass but it's so hard to let go and 'move on' like everyone says."

"I'm sorry," Alina said. She felt bad for Safi. *Every girl needs her mom*, she thought. She wanted to comfort Safi, but she had no idea what to say. A chill ran down her back. She didn't know what she'd do if her mom or dad passed away.

"I hope I get to meet your wise Nani," said Safi.

"You'll love her," said Alina.

Slowly, dot by dot, the butterfly on Alina's wrist took shape.

"I love it," she said, admiring her wrist. "Thank you! You're a talented artist just…," she stopped midway.

"That's Mom," said Safi. "I get it from her. I'm an aspiring artist."

"Sign your artwork," said Alina, stretching out her palm.

Safi dipped the toothpick into the bowl of henna and wrote her initials on Alina's wrist.

"All done. Now, don't stain your clothes," Safi warned. "Wait 'til the henna dries out then rinse it off with water."

After Safi finished her own henna design of branches of leaves with flowers, Alina washed her hand and examined her wrist. The bright orange butterfly shone. Very pleased, she took a picture with her phone and sent it to her friends, her parents, and to her nani.

Alina yearned to do something nice for her cousin. Suddenly she had a great idea. She'd give Safi a makeover! Lend some of her own clothes. That's what siblings do—they share stuff. Then they'd hang around in town like twinsies.

Alina went to her room, chose a pair of skinny jeans and a hoodie, and slipped them into a bag, pleased with her kindness.

Excited, she dashed down. "Look," she cried, showing her tattoo to Safi. "Looks so cool. Like it's ready to fly outside."

"I'm glad you like it," said Safi.

"Safi, I brought some of my comfy clothes for you," said Alina. She gave the bag to Safi.

"That's very nice of you, thank you," said Safi. She pulled each of the clothes out then folded them and put them back inside the bag. "I'm sorry, Alina. These just aren't my style. I prefer to wear long tunics in bright colors."

Alina's mouth hung open. Stunned. Speechless. Insulted.

1. ~~Wear hoodies and hang around like twinsies.~~

She crossed off another item on her dream list in her head. At this rate, nothing would be left.

"Fine," she said. She picked up the bag. It felt heavy. It wasn't just the bag, she felt herself grow heavy as well. As if she was sinking. **Down**, **down**, down, deep, deep, deep into the sea of darkness, feeling totally helpless.

She dashed upstairs to her room, dumped her bag, and slammed the door. All the excitement of the henna tattoo was gone, vanished. *Poof.*

She and Safi would never get along. They were too different. Like polar bears and penguins. If Alina was the North Pole, Safi was the South Pole. Total opposites. Like oil and water, they just couldn't mix. What would she do with her cousin for the rest of the holidays?

Alina sat on the edge of her bed, hugging her pillow, wanting to vent out her feelings. Unfortunately, both her best friends, Kim and Liam, were out of town. And she didn't feel like talking to her parents. They'd just side with Safi.

Desperate, she called her nani. But Nani was busy at the dentist and said she'd call back.

Alina gnawed the string of her hoodie waiting, waiting, until the phone rang.

"No cavities," Nani said proudly.

"That's because I eat all your chocolates," said Alina.

Nani said she really liked the henna design on Alina's wrist. She went on to say something about happiness was like a butterfly….

Alina waited for Nani to finish before she told her how hurt she felt at Safi's rejection of her clothes.

"Alee," said Nani, pausing to take a few long breaths. "Do the outer orange peel and the inside orange taste the same?"

Alina frowned. "Of course not. Nani, what do you mean?"

"Beta, Safi is Safi, and you are you. Our clothes are like the peel of an orange. They do not define us. The way we dress is not who we are inside, na?"

Alina agreed. "But we look so different," she said, biting her tongue. She remembered Nani's romantic story with Bapa. Nani had told Alina how different they both were at first, and yet they had loved each other.

"That's fine," said Nani. "We wear what we are comfortable with. Your mom usually wears pant suits, I prefer saris. Is that wrong?"

"No," said Alina, feeling a bit guilty. Once, she had freaked out when Nani dropped her at school in a salwar kameez. "Nani, you look like a queen."

The storm in Alina's mind calmed. She hung up, remembering what the lunch bully in her class had taught her. That it was okay to be different and not fit in sometimes. That she needed to accept herself. That she had to be brave enough to be herself. How did she forget all that?

It was okay if Safi wore a bright flashy salwar kameez or if she spoke in a weird accent. Nothing to be ashamed of. Nani was right. Safi was Safi and Alina was Alina. Safi did what she liked, and Alina would do what *she* liked, honoring both her Indian as well as her Canadian heritage.

Chapter 7
AT THE LIBRARY

Alina put on a pair of leggings with a graphic T-shirt and of course her fave hoodie. She stuffed her swimsuit and towel into her backpack and put on her soccer cap. Her parents had left for work. Today, she would take Safi to the library then cool off at the recreation center in their neighborhood.

It was a warm summer day. She walked Lux in the park. When she got home, she was relieved that Safi was wearing a simple tunic over flared Indian pants.

They walked down the hill to the Southwood Library.

"How nice that both the library and the pool are close by," said Safi.

Alina explained that Canada was divided into communities, so each community had its own library and recreation center.

"I like that about Canada," said Safi.

Inside the library, Safi's eyes glazed as she scanned the thousands of books on the shelves. Alina gave a quick tour showing Safi where to find what: picture books, nonfiction, and novels: mystery, fantasy, adventure, science fiction, and graphic novels.

"Wow!" cried Safi, looking dazed. Her voice rose. "How do I choose which books to borrow? I want them all."

"Shhh," said Alina, seeing Mrs. Aldrich, the librarian, raise her head and eyeing them. Safi was talking too loudly. This was a library.

Instead of taking the cue to be quiet, Safi marched forward to Mrs. Aldrich's desk.

O.M.G. Alina gaped.

"Hello, I'm Safi from Kenya," said Safi. Then she gripped Alina's arm. "And this is my cousin

Alina, who brought me here," said Safi. "I just love the smell of books. Isn't it delicious?"

Alina wanted to swallow herself whole.

Mrs. Aldrich smiled. "It sure is. I love working here. I'm glad you came. Welcome. Let me know if you need help."

They began to chat about Kenya.

Alina glanced back at the long lineup of people waiting to sign out their books. They were getting annoyed, but Safi didn't notice. She was chatting to the librarian as if they were best friends.

Alina pulled her hoodie over her head.

"What's the fee to borrow a book?" Safi asked.

"It's free," said Mrs. Aldrich.

"Free?" said Safi, as if she hadn't heard.

Mrs. Aldrich smiled and nodded.

Alina began to pray. *Safi, please don't make a scene.*

"What's the membership fee?" asked Safi.

"It's free," said Mrs. Aldrich, smiling again.

"Back home, we pay a membership fee, and then a fee for every book we borrow," said Safi. "How many books can I take?"

"As many as you want. There's no limit," said Mrs. Aldrich.

"Really?" said Safi, her eyes wide.

Alina stepped forward. "I'm sorry," she said, smiling apologetically to the librarian.

"I'm glad you brought Safi here," said Mrs. Aldrich.

Alina nodded and turned to Safi. "We'll use my library card. Go on, choose the books you like. I'll wait for you here."

Alina signed out a few interesting books on space, but when she went back to the librarian's desk, Safi wasn't there. Alina glanced at her watch. What was wrong? Safi was taking so long to choose her books.

Alina went to check and found Safi down on her knees, playing with a baby in a pram, gurgling and babbling, *muh-muh* and *bah-bah*.

"Are you done?" Alina asked.

"Not yet. Isn't Binh a darling?" said Safi. Alina nodded, glancing at the baby. "I'm playing with him so Ms. Nguyen can get some books," said Safi.

Alina wanted to say that they were running out of time to swim at the recreation center. Instead, she said, "I'll wait for you by the librarian's desk," and walked off.

After what seemed like hours later, Safi appeared with her zillion-dollar dimpled smile, her arms stacked with books. "Alina, Alina," she cried, "look what I got!" Safi couldn't even see her feet over the books she carried. Her toe caught on the carpet, and she tripped.

Boom! The books fell all over the floor.

People ran to help Safi.

Alina's cheeks warmed as she picked up some of the books. Why did Safi take so many?

It took forever for the poor librarian to sign off all of Safi's books. "Do you want to buy a bag?" she asked.

"No, thank you," said Safi before Alina could respond.

No way would all the books fit into Safi's bag. So, Alina had to stuff the rest of them into her backpack.

At last, they left the library. Alina's backpack was so heavy that every step she took felt like she was hauling a ton of bricks.

Safi went on and on about how excited she was to read so many books. "I'm going to sit outside on the patio in the sun with Lux, stretch my legs, sip spicy chai, and read all day long."

Alina nodded. They still had to climb a big hill to get to the recreation center. The load in her backpack made her back hurt. She felt a wetness crawl on her back. She was sweating.

"Alina, what do you think I should read first?" asked Safi. "*Because of Winn-Dixie* or the famous *Anne of Green Gables*?"

"My fave book is *Charlotte's Web*," said Alina. She had read the book a hundred times over.

"What about *A Wrinkle in Time*?" Safi asked.

Alina shrugged. "Sure." She was still embarrassed about the library; she didn't want to keep talking about books.

"No, no. I'll read the Nancy Drew series," said Safi. "I like how she solves mysteries and stuff. I can't wait to read about her adventures."

Alina's head hurt. "I'm tired," she said. "Let's axe swimming and go home."

"Sure," said Safi. "You rest. I'll catch up on my reading."

Alina nodded. But she didn't really want to rest. She vowed never to take Safi to the library again.

***

That evening, Alina waited for her mother to show up from work. When Safi went up to take a shower, Alina cornered her mother in the kitchen.

"Mom, I had a crazy day."

"I'm sorry," said Mom. She put her hand on Alina's arm.

"She's so loud," whispered Alina. "She made a scene at the library and then we didn't even make it to the rec center. I'm never taking her to the library again."

"Sweetie, Safi's only here for a month," said Mom.

"Thank goodness," said Alina.

Mom's face fell. "We must be kind, Alina, even if it's hard. Even if we think our guest is wrong.

This is Safi's first trip to Canada. What if you went to Nairobi and you acted like a Canadian there? How would Safi feel then?"

Alina nodded. But she knew she'd not act weird like Safi. Mom didn't really get it. She wasn't at the library to see what happened, so how would she understand?

Alina dashed upstairs to her room and called Nani, pouring out the event at the library with Safi.

Nani chuckled. "Sounds like you're having a different type of fun."

"Are you kidding?" said Alina.

"Alee, stop being a caterpillar. Safi's an extrovert and you're an introvert. Extroverts love talking and meeting new people, while introverts sometimes think more than they talk. You can still have fun together."

"The problem is she's weird," said Alina.

"I see," said Nani. "Alee, do you recall the strange tree we saw when hiking to Grassi Lake in Canmore last summer?"

"You mean the very weird tree?" said Alina.

"The very one," said Nani. "The branches grew every which way. You have that picture?"

Alina said she did.

"Look at it, Alee. Um…the branches of a tree grew in different directions, but the roots were one, na?"

"Fine," said Alina, wearily. "I'll try to be a butterfly, but Nani do come here as soon as you can."

Chapter 8

SURPRISES

The next morning when Alina came down, to her surprise, she saw Lux on Safi's lap. When did he bond with Safi?

"I hope you're feeling better," said Safi cheerfully.

Alina nodded and thanked her.

"Okay Lux, ready?" said Safi. "Do the penguin dance for Alina." Safi lay Lux down on the floor and began to count: "One, two, three." Then she clapped. "Go!"

Lux rose on his hind legs, sticking his paws out, wobbling all the way to the kitchen.

Alina laughed, clicking her phone to take pictures. She was impressed. "How did he learn that so quickly?"

"Magic," said Safi. She winked with an impish smile.

Alina was impressed.

She went to the kitchen and found another surprise. On the table lay fluffy white *pooris*, potato curry, and a warm golden Indian omelet folded in half next to a glass of milk. Safi had woken up early to cook breakfast. Guilt flooded through Alina. She should have cooked for their guest.

"This meal's fit for a queen. You didn't have to do this," she said.

"I wanted to. Eat, relax," Safi chirped cheerfully.

Alina sat down. She took the first bite of the omelet, already decided she wouldn't like it. But… it was flavorful. The poori were soft and the potato curry spicy and tangy.

She could make out the green chilies, spinach, cilantro, and green onions in the omelet. *How healthy*, she thought.

Safi joined her at the table.

"The omelet is yummy," Alina admitted.

"I'm glad you like it," said Safi.

Alina thought about showcasing the omelet in her *Yummy Tummy* show on YouTube. Her fans would love it. And before she knew it, she began to tell Safi how she'd won the *Junior Chef* contest on TV.

"That's amazing!" said Safi. "I had no idea you're a celebrity! I'll tell all my friends about my famous cousin."

Alina felt herself glow. She told Safi about her new school, the lunch bully, and how they had nailed him.

"How interesting," said Safi. "You should write a book about it. And if you do, I'll illustrate the pictures."

Alina laughed. Lux nudged her leg under the table. "Yes Lux, it's past your walkie time. Go find your leash." She rose and looked at Safi. "Want to walk him?"

"Sure," said Safi. "That'll be lovely."

They walked Lux along the gleaming Glenmore Reservoir, passing hikers, bikers, and joggers while the old steam train at Heritage Park whistled and chugged along.

Safi tucked her purse firmly under her arm. "Is it safe to walk here?" she asked.

"Of course," said Alina. "Why?"

"Just making sure. Pickpockets are common in some parts of Nairobi," said Safi.

"Yeah, that happens in big cities like New York, not here. Don't worry, you're totally safe here," said Alina.

"Some parts in Nairobi are quite dangerous. I don't take a purse or wear jewelry, not even a watch," said Safi.

"Then how do you buy anything?" asked Alina.

"I stash cash in my socks," said Safi.

Alina chuckled. She stopped to show the mountain peaks of the Rockies in the distance. They were on one side, Heritage Park and the tall skyscrapers of downtown were on the other side.

"Wow!" said Safi, clicking her camera.

"This lake has a thousand faces," said Alina. "In winter, it freezes into a skating rink. Then the warm chinook winds in the spring turn the lake into a checkerboard of blue and white. Both ice and water."

She showed Safi the video she'd taken of the lake on a warm spring day. The floating ice looked like a bouquet of crystal glass flowers. It broke apart slowly, crinkling, then gushed into the water.

"Wow!" said Safi again. "I wish we had winters. Kenya is sunny all year round with long and short rains."

"To be honest, I'd rather be in sunny Kenya," said Alina. "Lie on the beach, swim in the Indian ocean, and eat the exotic fruits you all talked about. It would be a dream to see the wildlife in the parks. Especially elephants. I love elephants, with their big flapping ears and long trunks."

"You don't need to go to the parks to see them. I always run into elephants on the Nairobi-Mombasa trip," said Safi.

"Lucky you. The fall here is chilly and the winter whitewashes everything. Brrr…sometimes it's so cold I literally stop to check if my nose is still there."

Safi laughed.

They stopped to let Lux pee.

"We should trade places," said Safi. "My dream is to play in the snow, build a snowman, and toboggan on the snow hills."

"Yup, it's a lot of fun," said Alina. "Also skiing and skating, then roasting marshmallows over fire."

"Ducks!" cried Safi suddenly. She clicked her camera as a family of ducks glided past in the water.

Farther along the trail, they ran into a gaggle of geese hissing and honking, blocking their path.

"Help!" cried Safi, looking around for help.

The geese honked louder.

"Calm down," said Alina. "We'll walk around them."

"No way. I'm not moving." Safi's gaze was glued to the geese.

"C'mon," said Alina. "Don't you come from the land of lions?"

Safi stood rooted, her eyes wide.

"Here." Alina caught Safi's hand and led her away from the geese onto the grass.

They chuckled.

"You're a brave one," said Safi.

Funny, thought Alina. She thought it was quite the opposite. She'd never be able to live in a place with street thieves and limited water and power.

As they walked back home, Alina thought to herself that Safi may be weird, but she was also weirdly funny too. Alina liked that.

Chapter 9

STAMPEDE

"Stampede's here! High five." Alina raised her hand.

Lux rose on his hind legs and offered his paw to her.

Alina wore her stampede outfit, a western, blue-checkered shirt over distressed jeans. She put on her cowboy hat and cried, "Yahoo!" swirling Lux's leash in the air like a cowboy's lasso catching runaway cattle.

She was looking forward to the new rides. Last year, the Ferris wheel with her friends was the best. She remembered the swirling, spinning, laughter, and the insane screaming: "Let-me-off, let-me-off, let-me-off!" There would be new food options too. Last time she and her friends ate fried Oreo cookies, a finger-licking delight.

This summer her friends were away—Kim was visiting her grandparents in Korea and Liam was camping with his family in the mountains. Alina was stuck with her cousin.

Oh well, she thought. Some company is better than none. To avoid any goof-ups, she'd prep Safi about the Stampede.

She and Lux went down to find Safi busy reading. She wore a bright purple salwar kameez with intricate mirror work that reflected a hundred faces of a frowning Alina.

The Indian outfit on the Stampede ground would stick out like a red flag. Alina could not take Safi like that. No way. Not in a zillion years.

She began to tell Safi about the festival while she tried to think of what to do. "The Stampede is the greatest outdoor show in the world. It's held every year in July."

"I'm lucky, I came at the right time," said Safi.

Alina went on: "There's rodeo, chuckwagon races, and bull fights. There are rides, yummy food, and games galore."

"Sounds like *fun* galore. Will we go?" Safi asked.

"You bet. Today we'll watch the parade on TV. We'll go to the festival tomorrow, it's kid's day," said Alina. "Um…the festival shows the Wild West and the cowboy life out on the prairies. Everyone in the city dresses up like cowboys and cowgirls for a week. Even people in restaurants and offices."

"Oh," said Safi. "I don't find jeans comfortable. Can I wear a jean skirt?"

"Perfecto," said Alina. "I've a jean jacket to go with the skirt, and you can wear Mom's cowboy hat."

"Thanks," said Safi. "That will be lovely," she said.

Alina felt the load in her mind lift off. "There'll be free breakfast at different places all over Calgary," she said.

"Free?" Safi's dark eyes widened. "For everybody?"

"Yup," said Alina. "Tom, Dick, Harry, and their dogs and cats."

"But what if they run out of food?" asked Safi.

"They don't," said Alina. "They never do."

They sat with Lux in the family room and watched the Stampede parade on TV. It showed marching bands, so many floats and dances by different cultural groups, politicians, and leaders dressed like cowboys rode horses.

Safi clapped. "I've not seen anything like this," she said.

Early the next day, Alina thought Safi looked fabulous in the jean skirt and a white button-down shirt. She even wore a thick brown leather belt, and Alina's jean jacket.

"You look great," said Alina. Safi was tall and elegant in any outfit, Alina realized.

"Thanks," said Safi with a bashful smile.

Dad dropped them to the Stampede grounds. He gave them a couple of hours and said he'd wait for them by the entrance. There were so many people and loud music blared. It was easy to get lost. Alina caught Safi's hand, and they walked together.

"First, let's go for the free breakfast," said Safi.

It was a long winding line. Alina sighed. She'd skip it but….

They lined up to get the free pancakes.

After an endless wait, they got a stack of pancakes topped with golden maple syrup.

"Yum, yum," said Safi, gorging herself on the pancakes one by one.

"Shhh," said Alina, checking the crowd.

Safi seemed oblivious to her shushing. "I've had pancakes before, but not with this yum-yum sauce," she said.

"It's maple syrup," said Alina. "It's Canadian."

"It's amazing. Can I get more?" said Safi.

Alina was anxious to get to the rides, but she nodded.

At last, when the pancake fiesta was finally over, Alina linked her arm into Safi's. "Let's check out the rides," she said.

"I'm too full," said Safi. "Later, okay?"

Alina agreed grudgingly. "Okay, let's check out the games."

They skipped from stall to stall. There was Whack-a-Mole, Ring Tossing, Breaking Plates, Bean Bag Tossing, and Bottle Fishing.

Alina looked at the huge stuffed white tiger hanging in the game stall and was tempted to try out her luck. She checked her wallet. "I can play three games."

"Don't," said Safi. "You'll never win. They make it too hard. It's a business, they just want your money."

"I play for fun," said Alina.

She played three games but lost all of them. "C'mon, let's check out the rides," she said.

They watched the Zipper, a fast flippy ride. It was noisy with the riders screaming loudly as they flipped.

"It doesn't look safe," said Safi.

The next ride was the Mega Drop. It brought the riders up about forty meters above the ground and then dropped them.

"Looks scary," said Safi.

"But we'll see the skyscrapers of Calgary from the sky," said Alina.

"I'm sorry," said Safi. "You can't pay me enough."

They walked to the Skyscraper Ride. It made the riders spin round and round.

"Let's go for it?" said Alina.

"I'll pass. I get sick on planes," said Safi. "I'm sorry, these rides aren't really for me. You pay through your teeth and the fun's over in a few minutes."

Alina made a face. "You've got to spend if you want fun in life," she said.

"You can go. I'll take your picture," said Safi.

Alina shook her head. What fun was it to ride all by yourself? "Let's go to the kid's section," she suggested.

They stopped at the Merry-Go-Round.

"This is a gentle ride," said Alina.

Safi shrugged. "Okay, let's try," she said.

The line-up for the ride was superlong. At last, it was their turn when Safi suddenly ran to the side and began to throw up.

Dear me. People stared at them. Alina died a thousand deaths. Why did Safi eat so many of the free pancakes? Alina offered Safi a tissue to wipe her mouth.

Alina's excitement had fizzled. It was time to head home.

It took some time to find Dad. As the girls walked toward the exit, Safi stopped to read aloud the poster for *Tandoori Chicken Poutine* on the food truck. It showed a picture of fries with butter chicken sauce.

"Poutine?" Safi cried in an excited voice. "My brothers told me about this!"

Poutine was Alina's favorite too. "Basically, it's fries with gravy and cheese curds, but looks like they've improvised it with butter chicken sauce," she said, her tastebuds clicking.

Safi took out her phone and took a few pictures of the food truck. "I'd love to try it," she said.

Alina could not believe it. "But aren't you sick?" she said.

"I'm better now," said Safi. "In fact, I'm hungry. I emptied everything in my stomach."

Dad told them to sit while he placed the order.

They all sat on the bench to eat. Safi took pictures of the poutine and sent it off to her brothers.

She ate the first mouthful. "Ah! This is heavenly," she said.

"Yes, richness in every bite," said Alina, her mouth full.

At last, she had found one thing in common with her cousin: they were both foodies.

"Alina, I can show you some African meals you may want to add to your YouTube show," said Safi.

"Terrific!" said Alina. "Let's do that after soccer camp."

On the way back home, Dad asked Alina in the car why she was quiet.

"I'm tired," she said, closing her eyes.

She could not help feeling disappointed and sorry for herself for missing all the rip-roaring rides at the Stampede. If only her friends, Kim and Liam, were here. If only she had gone with them to the Stampede. They would all have had a great time. If only…if only….

Chapter 10
SOCCER

Late that evening, Alina sang as she packed. "Ready, ready, ready. To kick and pass and dribble and score. Yay!" She was off to a soccer camp the next day with Safi in Canmore for a week.

"I'll miss you buddy," said Alina, cuddling Lux.

He climbed into her lap and rubbed his furry cheek against hers. Then suddenly he went still, his ears perking up.

"What's wrong?" said Alina. She heard muffled sounds coming from Safi's room. *Safi must miss her mom*, thought Alina. "C'mon buddy, let's check her out."

She knocked on the slightly ajar door of the guest room and went inside.

Safi was bent double on the bed, gripping the pillow.

Alina sat with Lux on the bed and put her arm around Safi. "I'm sorry. Can I help you?"

Lux stretched out and began to lick Safi's wet face.

Safi smiled through her tears. "What a good friend you are."

It turned out that Safi didn't want to go to the soccer camp. She said that she played kickball with her older brothers in their back alley every day, but only for fun. The soccer camp would have a lot of really good players, and Safi wasn't sure she'd fit in.

Alina felt bad for Safi. "Don't worry, we'll axe the camp," she said, crossing off yet another item in her dream list in her head.

5. ~~Soccer Camp. Yippee!~~

Alina didn't feel super bad for axing the soccer camp. Besides, taking Safi to the camp might just be an embarrassment for both.

***

The next day, Mom cancelled the soccer camp and signed them up for soccer practice with Darius, the coach at the community center. It was good for beginners as well as strong players, so Alina told Safi she'd be okay.

"You'll like Darius. He's cool," Alina assured Safi. He always praised Alina for being a fast runner and for her killer kick.

Safi brought out her sneakers. "They need a bath," she said with a chuckle. She drenched a rag with soap and water and began to scrub them.

Alina looked at the wrinkled, worn-out sneakers. "Are you sure you can play in these?" she asked.

"Aha, they'll be spanking new in a few minutes," said Safi.

***

The air was crisp and cool and the grass on the soccer field shone with the morning dew. Coach

Darius greeted the girls with fist bumps and high fives as he always did.

Safi caught on quickly and did the same.

The girls joined the other players on the grass. Darius explained how warm-up drills improve soccer skills. In the first drill, they had to race around the field three times.

Alina braced to start. She was a fast runner and usually came first or second in the race. Coach Darius blew the whistle. The race began. Alina took the lead in round one but, to her immense surprise, Safi zoomed past her like a rocket in the second half.

"Woo!" Coach Darius cheered for Safi.

Alina felt a burn inside as she finished after Safi. A tiny tear slipped out of the corner of her eye. At home she had felt alienated, but soccer was one place where she always shone. She was disappointed in herself. Quickly, she rubbed the wetness with the back of her hand, as if wiping away dust.

"Good job," she told Safi.

"Thanks," said Safi with a bashful smile.

Next, Coach Darius showed the players three new moves: the toe bounce, crossover, and the three-sixty spin. He passed the balls to every player and told them to practice the moves until they were ready to play the game.

Both Alina and Safi did all three moves without any help from the coach.

"Game time," cried Coach Darius. He divided the players into two teams and handed out red and blue bands. Alina was in team blue, Safi in team red. They'd play defense on opposing teams.

Coach Darius blew the whistle. The game began. Alina got the ball and dribbled it across the field with Safi tailing her closely. Safi caught up to Alina. Alina paused momentarily, using the sole of her foot to protect the ball, but Safi hustled until she managed to wrangle the ball out.

She faked a pass then did the famous three-sixty spin, kicking the ball to a midfield player on her team, who shot and scored. Safi got an assist.

Alina pressed her lips tight. She was happy for Safi, but her heart sank. Soccer was her passion.

Her journal showed that she wanted to be the next Christine Sinclair, the famous Canadian soccer star.

Alina would not give up. She hustled and managed to get the ball back. She would not let it go and controlled it close to her feet. She dribbled quickly, saving their goalie while her team cheered.

Unfortunately, on the next play, a player from the red team scored.

Coach Darius blew the whistle. He changed positions. This time both Alina and Safi were forwards.

The girls faced each other in the center circle of the field. Safi smiled.

Alina couldn't return the smile. She felt jittery, her heart bouncing. *Thump! Thump! Thump!* Like the soccer ball. Sweat trickled down her back. She'd get the ball. She had to.

Yes! she thought, as she dragged it back with her toe. Then she ran, dribbling the ball across the field, moving side to side with it. She wondered why Safi had not caught up with her.

A player from the red team tried to get the ball from her, but Alina deftly dragged it to her other foot and changed direction. She dribbled it all the way to the net then gave her killer kick.

She scored!

Her team went wild with excitement, some of them fell over their knees and caught her arm, cheering.

Alina was surprised to find Safi was cheering for her too. She smiled but a niggling doubt ran through her head. Did Safi deliberately slow down to let her score?

Alina realized that yes, very likely, Safi had. Would she have done the same for Safi? Give up the ball to let Safi score?

Alina wasn't sure. She felt intimidated by Safi, who was so good even though she'd never been to a soccer class before.

After the game, when the players were changing in the locker room, she confronted Safi.

"Why did you let me score?" Alina asked.

Safi shook her head as if to deny it, then broke into a slow smile. "'Cause you're not only my cousin but my friend too. Friends help each other. Didn't Charlotte in *Charlotte's Web* use her web-spinning skills to save Wilbur's life? I wanted to make you happy."

The story reminded Alina of unlikely friendships.

Whoever thought a pig and a spider could be friends? She and Safi may be as different as a polar bear and a penguin, but they could be friends.

"Thanks," she gripped Safi's arm. "That was very sweet of you. But please don't do that again. I'd like to win with my own skills and effort. If I lose, so be it. I'll have to learn not to be a sore loser. Promise you won't let me win, and I'll promise to be gracious even when I lose."

"Pinky promise," said Safi, and they locked their pinky fingers.

The day turned out to be not so bad after all. Not everything in Alina's dream list had worked, but the summer holidays with her weird cousin were beginning to feel like if she'd stretch her arm a little higher, she might just touch cloud nine.

Chapter 11
DAD'S BIRTHDAY

Nani called to say she'd be making a surprise visit on Dad's birthday the next day.

"Yay!" cried Alina.

She ran and told Mom and Safi. Mom said after Dad's birthday, they'd take Nani and Safi to Banff.

At night, Alina flipped through her recipe book in her room, trying to choose what meal to cook on Dad's birthday between two of his fave dishes.

"Help me, Lux," she said. "Wag your tail if you like the meal. Number one: coconut chicken curry, or *kuku paka* as we say in Gujarati." She looked at Lux.

He wagged his tail.

"Number two: beans in coconut or *bharazi*?"

Lux wagged his tail again. She laughed aloud.

The phone rang again. Much to her surprise, it was from Emily, one of the four popular girls in her class. She invited Alina to a bowling party tomorrow afternoon.

Alina was surprised. She wasn't close to Emily or her friends and was flattered at being invited. No way would she take Safi with her. They would not understand her cousin. And Safi probably wouldn't like them, either. Alina decided she'd bike to the club by herself. Safi could stay at home with Lux.

★★★

The next morning, Alina found a bowl of strange-looking fruits on the table. Lux sniffed and began to bark.

"Not for you," said Alina.

"They're tropical fruits," cried Safi, her eyes sparkling with excitement.

Alina nodded. "Mom must have ordered them from the specialty store for Dad's birthday."

Safi squealed in delight. She put her nose right up to the strange fruits, breathing in. "Ahhh, smells sooo good. I feel like I'm home." She named them all—mango, guava, passion fruit, and custard apple or sitaphal.

"What would you like to try?" Safi asked.

Alina picked up the custard apple. "This doesn't look like an apple. Looks more like an artichoke. How do you eat it?"

"My mom's favorite," said Safi. "It's packed with nutrients and other things to fight cancer. They're super healthy." She checked the fruit's ripeness with her hand then pulled it apart. "Here, try it. Scoop out the white flesh with a spoon."

Alina bit into the flesh of the sitaphal. It was sweet and creamy, so flavorful until—oh, her teeth crunched on something hard. "What the?" The juice dribbled down her chin.

"Oops, spit it out, spit it out," Safi cried. "I forgot to say it has seeds."

"*Now* you tell me," Alina said.

"I'm sorry," Safi said and burst into a fit of giggles.

Alina laughed as well, but Safi could not stop giggling.

"Hey, I want more of that." Alina ate more of the fruit, this time spitting out all the watermelon-like black seeds. "I can't believe how yummy this is," she said.

Suddenly a great idea sparked for her dad's birthday. She would use these fruits to make a fruit pizza.

She arranged the fruits on the fruit pizza in her mind. It would be a delicious, sumptuous surprise. Dad, Mom, and Safi would love it and Nani would beam with pride. Perfecto!

There were so many events Alina was looking forward to—the bowling party with her classmates, then Dad's birthday, then the trip to Banff. Yippee!

Chapter 12
BOWLING PARTY

Alina met Emily, Ava, and Lily, at the bowling club that afternoon. They all wore the same stretchy clothes in pink.

Alina felt out of place in her old jeans and blue hoodie.

Emily hugged her, saying, "I'm so glad you made it even though I invited you late."

Ava said, "Mia's away and we wanted a foursome."

Alina felt warm. Would she have been invited if Mia was here? It didn't seem so.

She suddenly wanted to leave.

"Listen up," said Emily. "We're going to play goofy bowling." She flicked her ponytail, tied in an enormous pink bow. "Each player has to come up with a funny way to strike the pins."

Ava and Lily thrust their chests forward and back with funny hand gestures, yelling gibberish. Emily laughed, but Alina couldn't bring herself to.

What would Safi do? she wondered. Safi would have done something unexpected and made her laugh. Alina wished Safi was here.

Next, they played bowling backwards. The girls turned around and rolled the ball blindly between their legs. Then they took a long break for burgers and fries and milkshakes.

Next, they played granny bowling, rolling the ball using both hands, laughing. Alina didn't find it funny. She glanced at the watch. It was already three o'clock.

"I'm sorry. I have to go," she said. "It's my dad's birthday."

Emily pouted. "You can't. The fun just started."

"C'mon, we're counting on you," said Lily.

"Yeah, don't be a party pooper," said Ava.

"Fine," said Alina, worried. She still had to make the fruit pizza.

After the next round, they took another break for nachos.

By the time the party ended, it was five. Alina had overstayed. Her nani would be at her house by now. She thanked the girls and rode home on her bike as quickly as she could.

★★★

Alina barged home to find Safi and Nani in the kitchen, chatting and laughing. Safi was peeling potatoes and Nani was shelling peas. Just the sight of them together hurt Alina. Like she'd been punched in the gut by a hundred-pound gorilla. She always explored new recipes with Nani.

Nani hugged Alina. "Sorry beta, my hands are dirty," she said.

Alina already wanted to leave, but she had to make the fruit pizza. "Where are the tropical fruits?" she asked. Safi pointed to the squashed fruit pieces by the sink. "We made a tropical smoothie."

Alina stared at the squashed fruit, feeling like her heart was squashed as well. She could not speak.

Her plan to surprise Dad with the fruit pizza was ruined. Ruined by her coming late after the stupid bowling party that wasn't any fun anyway. It was her own fault.

"Alee, you look pale. Are you okay?" Nani asked.

Alina nodded. She managed to say, "I overate at the party. I need a nap," she said and took off before she had a meltdown in front of them.

Lux followed her to her room. He seemed to sense that she'd had a bad day. He nestled near her on the bed and began to lick her wet face. *Don't cry. Please don't cry.* He licked her face again and again, a hundred kisses, until she calmed down.

Then he dove down and returned, his squeaky squirrel, his fave toy clamped in his mouth. He wanted to play tug-of-war.

"Ready, set, tug." Alina tried and tried to pull the toy from his mouth, but Lux wouldn't let go.

They played again and again. "You win," she said. "You're the champ."

Finally, feeling more herself, she rose. She did not want to make another big mistake and ruin Dad's special day. "Okay, Lux, let's go."

They joined Nani and Safi in the kitchen.

"Safi's helping me cook a special meal for Dad," said Nani.

"It's an African dish called *irio*," said Safi.

"I've never had it before," said Alina. "I look forward to trying it."

As soon as Dad stepped inside, they began to sing "Happy Birthday," followed by hugs.

Alina found the rest of the evening a painful blurry blob, but she stayed calm. They all sat at the table to eat.

"I didn't know a vegetable dish can be so yummy," said Dad, taking another helping of irio.

"Thank you," said Safi, glowing with pride.

"It's tasty," said Alina, feeling her heart shrink. It *was* nice. But she'd wanted to share her own surprise, too.

The dinner ended with tall glasses of tropical fruit smoothie floating with almonds and pistachios.

"This is the best smoothie I've had," said Mom.

Everyone agreed, even Alina. *If only she had made the fruit pizza,* she thought. *It would have been delicious, too.*

Nani whispered in Alina's ear. "Beta, you look tired. You okay?"

Alina nodded and forced a big smile. She did not want Nani to worry about her.

That night in the deep blackness of her room, Alina cuddled Lux, reflecting on her big mistake. How dumb was she not to put her foot down and leave the bowling party earlier?

She snuggled close to Lux, taking in his body heat. Lux, at least, could make her feel better.

Chapter 13
THE SEARCH: DAY 1

Alina woke up early feeling blah. As if a zillion bees were buzzing inside her head. She had lost herself. She needed some "me time" to sort herself out, to pull herself up by her bootstraps before she went on the trip to Banff with her family tomorrow.

"Want a new sniffing adventure?" she asked.

Lux leapt up in the air.

She'd take Lux to a new off-leash dog park. Her parents had left to go to work. She wrote a note for Nani and Safi and left.

The dog park was at the west end of the Glenmore Reservoir where the Elbow River ran through the swampy marsh. It was a pleasant morning. The sun shone in a cloudless sky and the air was filled with scents of wildflowers and endless chirping. Alina heard chickadees and woodpeckers.

They passed by hikers and bikers and joggers. Lux had the time of his life sniffing at several gopher holes and chasing the poor crows resting on the grass. The rabbits were too fast for him, but when a squirrel darted, Lux ran after it. The squirrel disappeared behind a wall made of rocks. Lux put his nose right next to the wall, waiting for the squirrel to come out.

"No Lux, no," warned Alina. Lux had a strong drive for squirrels. She always rewarded him with treats for not chasing them, but today she had forgotten to pack any.

Suddenly, the squirrel snuck out from his hideout and ran. Lux bolted after him like a rocket. Alina ran after them, but they sprinted into the woods and out of her sight.

"Lux! Lux!" she cried frantically, running as fast as she could, sometimes turning right, sometimes left around the trees, her heart racing.

There was no sign of Lux anywhere. Alina's stomach tangled into knots.

Eventually, she reached a barbed wire fence before the Weaselhead Flats. It was a vast wilderness full of beavers, muskrats, coyotes. A shiver ran through her. What if they caught Lux?

She called her parents.

Mom said she'd come right away. Dad called animal services to report a lost dog. Unfortunately, Lux did not have a chip for pet identification. Next, Alina called Nani and told her what had happened. Nani said to wait for her at the entrance of the park.

Very soon, Nani came with Safi. A teary Alina ran into Nani's arms.

"We'll find him," said Nani. "Where could he have gone?"

"*Hakuna matata*, no worries," said Safi. "I posted a picture of Lux on Instagram. Someone is sure to spot him."

Nani coaxed Alina to eat the egg sandwiches she'd made. They began to look for Lux, calling for him loudly. They stopped every jogger, hiker, and biker in the park, telling them to please watch out for a lost dog and gave them the number to call.

They reached the rock wall where the squirrel first hid.

No Lux.

They split up, Safi and Alina went together and Nani by herself, and combed the area.

No Lux.

Very shortly, Dad showed up in his doctor's blue scrubs and Mom in a business suit. Alina was relieved to see them, and they both gave her big hugs. Now they could cover more ground to search for Lux. She had been wrong about not feeling included in her family. They were there for each other when they needed it.

Dad said not to call out Lux's name out when searching. "He's in flight mode, he may perceive that as a threat."

They split up, looking for Lux in different directions for hours until the sky grew dark and there was lightning and thunder followed by a heavy rain. Alina and her family were forced to leave.

★★★

Back home, Dad cancelled the trip to Banff the next day. Safi printed a hundred flyers that said "Missing Dog" with a picture of Lux.

The girls knelt on the floor in Alina's bedroom and prayed together until midnight.

"I know how hard this is," Safi said. "Lux is not just a pet, he's family."

Alina nodded. "What if he's hurt?" she asked. "He'll be cold and hungry and drenched. And scared! He's so scared of thunder," Alina realized with horror, "he hides under my bed!"

Safi held Alina's hand. "Lux is smart. He'll find shelter somewhere tonight, and we'll find him tomorrow."

Alina hoped she was right. "I'm sorry we had to cancel the Banff trip," she said.

"Bah," Safi dismissed it. "What matters is we find Lux."

Alina nodded. Safi was a real friend.

"I'm sorry," said Alina. "When you first came, I was upset that my parents doted on you so much. Also, you appeared so different I thought we would never get along. I'm so glad you came," she said, squeezing Safi's hand.

Safi returned the squeeze. "Likewise, I'm very glad to be here with you."

"I now get the African saying on the cloth you gave," said Alina. *When trouble comes, it's your family that supports you.* She wished she had understood it when Safi had given it to her mom. She wished she'd known what a special gift it really was.

Alina rose to look for the shell necklace that Safi had given her. She'd wear it tomorrow while they looked for Lux. She put the necklace under her pillow, hoping and praying that the magic in it would rub off.

Chapter 14
THE SEARCH: DAY 2

Early the next day, Alina put on the necklace and woke Safi up.

"This necklace is magical. It gave me a great idea," said Alina. Excited, she shared her plan to set up a feeding station for Lux in the park.

"Brilliant idea," said Safi. "Let's take his fave toy and other stuff too and use their scents to lure him out."

"But where do we set them up?" asked Alina.

They thought about it for a few minutes.

"How 'bout the rock wall where Lux first saw the squirrel?" said Safi.

"Perfect," said Alina. She packed some treats, Lux's squeaky squirrel toy, and his tattered blanket.

She shared her plan with Nani and her parents before they left for work. Nani said she'd join them at the park after her doctor's appointment.

Dad warned, "Be extra careful if you spot Lux. He'll be confused and scared. Stay calm."

The girls ate a quick breakfast, took the scents for Lux, snacks, and water bottles, and left for the park.

The sun was rising as Alina set up the feeding station by the rock wall. The girls split up and went in different directions to search for Lux.

At lunchtime, they met Nani at the park. They checked the food station. The blanket and the doggy treats seemed untouched.

"Do you think he's alive?" Alina asked, bursting into tears.

Nani pulled Alina close. "Beta, I think he's hiding and scared to come out. Hunger will force him out soon."

They ate snacks and resumed the search for Lux.

In the evening, Alina's parents joined Nani and the girls. Once again, in a couple of hours, the sky darkened, and the wind started to gust. A severe thunderstorm warning came through on their phones, forcing them to call off the search.

That night as the girls lay down to sleep, Alina thanked Safi. "I feel so bad for ruining your holiday," she said. "Here you are looking for Lux every day instead of sightseeing."

"A great holiday is being with you," said Safi.

"Losing Lux is so hard," said Alina. "I can't imagine how hard it must have been for you when your mom passed away."

Safi nodded. She was quiet for a long moment. "I felt like I could not go on without my mom. I did have Dad, my brothers, Dadi, and plenty of friends, but I felt alone. Like a part of me died when Mom died." She paused. "Now with all of you here, I learned that grief and joy can coexist. I'm trying to slowly crawl out of my cocoon and be a butterfly," she whispered, smiling her dimpled smile.

Alina hugged Safi. "I care for you. I'm here for you," said Alina.

"Thank you Alee," said Safi. "I care for you too and will always stand by you," she said in a tear-jerky voice. "We will find Lux. Miracles can and do happen. We will find our Lux."

Chapter 15

THE SEARCH: DAY 3

Alina and Safi woke up the next day with red blotches all over their faces and arms and legs.

"Mosquito bites," said Alina, scratching her arm.

"Canadian mosquitoes are more vicious than African ones," Safi said with a chuckle.

They began to count their bites, trying to figure out who had the most.

"Fifteen," said Alina.

"Nineteen," said Safi.

Alina's parents had left for work. Nani was preparing breakfast when Alina's phone rang.

"Hi, is this the number to call for a lost dog?" asked a man.

Alina's heart whooped. "Yes, yes, it is!"

The man went on, "My name's Jason Smith. I'm calling the number from the flyer. Me and my dog were having a picnic at the park when a stray dog came by. I gave him some food and he licked it up and wants more. Looks like the lost cockapoo on the flyer."

"Oh my god, oh my god!" Alina cried aloud. "It might be Lux. Please, please Mr. Smith hold on to him. I'll be there right away."

The man said he'd wait by the swamp at Glenmore Park.

Alina broke the news to Nani and Safi. Nani said to leave at once. She'd follow behind as she couldn't walk as fast.

It began to drizzle, but the girls didn't care. They ran as fast as they could all the way to Glenmore Park. They found the swamp; it was close to the feeding station.

A few feet away, Alina saw the man in a raincoat holding an umbrella over his dog. Yes, the other dog was Lux all right.

Alina's heart trilled with joy. There he stood, scrawny little Lux, his fur muddy brown, his chocolate eyes big and wide. She had to be very careful not to scare him.

She planned a strategy with Safi to catch Lux. Slowly, Alina crab-walked sideways, very slowly toward Lux while Safi did the same on the opposite end.

Alina's breath came in ragged gasps. With every footstep, fear surged. What if he ran away? *Please don't run, please, please.* Sweat trickled down her temples beneath her hoodie.

Then in one fluid motion, she dropped on the ground and scooped Lux up gently into her arm, her heart pounding with fierce joy.

They lay on the muddy earth while the rain poured. "I have you now, I have you. You're safe and sound," she said, tears streaking down her face. "I love you, boy, I love you. We're joined at the hip, right?"

Safi came closer and stroked Lux. "Don't you ever go chasing squirrels again."

Alina turned to the man. "Thank you! Thank you! I can't thank you enough."

Then Nani arrived, and she was all smiles when she saw Lux.

Back home, Alina fed Lux and gave him a warm bath while Safi rang the vet and asked him to come to their house.

The vet examined Lux and said his leg was bruised, but it would heal. Thankfully, there were no major problems except for some weight loss.

Alina hugged Safi. She held the necklace around her neck. "This is magical. It's the best gift. I will treasure it forever. You were right, Safi. Miracles do happen. Lux is our miracle dog!"

Chapter 16

FUN GALORE

Yippee! Alina's best friends, Kim and Liam, were back in town. She invited them to meet Safi. They were going to have a water balloon party in her backyard!

It turned out to be the perfect hot summer day, so hot that you could fry an egg on the sidewalk. Kim showed them wonderful photos of temples and beaches she had seen in Korea. "But my best time was meeting my grandparents," she said.

Liam talked about his camping trip in the mountains—how he'd gaze at the sky every night and eat gooey s'mores.

Alina explained to Safi what s'mores were.

Then Safi told them how Lux got lost. "My best part of the holiday," she said, "was finding Lux and seeing the joy in Alina's face."

They all turned to Alina.

Alina said, "My holiday was magical because Safi came to visit."

They played duck, duck, splash, tossing the water balloons and laughing. Then they had an epic water balloon fight and ate seaweed cookies and honey-butter chips that Kim had brought from Korea.

"Riddle time," said Liam, rubbing his palms together.

Everybody turned to look at Liam. He always came up with interesting facts.

"Clouds weigh a zillion pounds," said Liam. "Some of them are like as heavy as a hundred elephants. So how do they stay up in the sky?"

"Well, well," said Safi thoughtfully. "A helium balloon also floats in the sky."

"I can't think," said Alina. "My head's in the clouds." Everybody giggled.

Liam glanced at Kim. Her father was Mr. Scientific and knew all the answers.

"Hmmm," said Kim. "Is it something to do with different densities?"

"Right," said Liam. "The clouds are surrounded by warm air, which is less dense than cold air, and that lifts up the clouds."

And just like how all good things come to an end, Kim and Liam's parents came to pick them up.

"Hey, I have a riddle before you leave," said Alina. "Why can't penguins and polar bears be friends?" she asked.

"Easy-peasy," said Liam. "'Cause they live on opposite ends of earth and will never meet each other."

★★★

Mom and Dad took a delayed week off work to take Safi to Banff and sightseeing around Calgary. Nani extended her holiday as well. Alina drew up a list of all the fun places to visit.

1. Grassi Lake in Canmore to pay homage to the very weird tree.
2. Johnston Canyon at Banff National Park, then the Lake Agnes Teahouse Trek, a soak in the hot springs, and a gondola ride on the amazing Rocky Mountain ranges.
3. Climb 726 steps at the Calgary Tower.
4. Canada geese at Princess Island Park for "Safi-goosebumps" and laughter.
5. Somehow get Safi on some of the rides at the Calgary Heritage Park.
6. Explore Calgary's Red Mile where fans of Calgary Flames hockey team flock to cheer the team.

The week literally flew by. *Time really does fly when you're having fun*, thought Alina.

Before she left for Edmonton, Nani pulled Alina aside and gave her a big hug. She told her how proud she was that Alina had become her very own butterfly. "Sometimes," Nani said, "we may not have it all together, but together, we have it all."

Chapter 17
GOOD-BYE

In the last week of Safi's stay, Alina interviewed Safi every day for her *Yummy Tummy* food channel. Every day Safi cooked a new Indian African dish. Every day, the girls walked Lux, played ball, and watched TV.

Safi fell in love with ice hockey, and they watched all the past Calgary Flames games. "I must learn to skate," said Safi. She tried to fake skate and skidded on the floor with a bump and a fall. Alina had a great laugh.

Safi's other love was her yum-yum sauce. She poured maple syrup on every dish.

Alina watched a popular old Hindi movie with Safi called *Mughal-e-Azam* and found herself crying loudly when the actress was going to be entombed alive.

Safi hugged Alina. "It's just a story," she said, "and a fake one." Alina laughed and wiped her tears.

Alina and Safi may not be twinsies, but they did have a fun-filled summer after all.

Now, Alina waited with Lux, her parents, and Safi at the departure level in Calgary airport. In 65 minutes, that is 3,900 seconds, Safi would depart on a long flight back home to Kenya. Nobody talked. Even Lux was quiet.

Alina looked around her at the families hugging and kissing each other, some crying, some laughing nervously. She swallowed. Good-byes were hard. Especially when her heart was packed with emotions and memories.

It was good-bye time. Safi hugged Alina's parents, then Lux, who rose on his hind legs and licked Safi's cheeks again and again. The last and longest hug was reserved for Alina.

"Write to me, Alee," said Safi. "A friend's a friend no matter how far they are. Cheerio, au revoir."

Alina wanted to add that a friend's a friend no matter how different they are. But to her surprise, even though she *never ever* cried in public, she found tears trailing down her face like a leaky faucet.

It was a bittersweet farewell. She'd miss Safi, but guess what? Next summer her parents had agreed that she would visit Safi in Kenya. *Yippee!*

Also, she and Safi had already made their dream list of fun things to do in Kenya.

1. **Visit the open-air markets for tropical fruits, especially sitaphal and make a delicious tropical fruit pizza.**

2. **See baby elephants at the elephant orphanage and learn the dangers they face.**

3. Tour Masai Mara Reserve to see elephants, lions, hippos, rhinos, leopards....
4. Hot balloon ride to see wildlife at Nairobi National Park.
5. Experience village life with Safi's dadi, milk the cows, draw water from the wells....
6. Visit the Kibera slums to experience everyday life in the informal settlement.
7. Feed giraffes at the Giraffe Centre.

Oh boy! Alina couldn't wait.

THE END

ACKNOWLEDGMENTS

Cliché or not, it really does take a village to write a story and get it published. Writing this story has been bittersweet. Lux slept right by my feet as I click-clacked the first draft of this story. He could not wait for the book to be published and crossed the Rainbow Bridge to Doggie Heaven, leaving behind loving memories.

Thank you, young readers, for reading the book. Thank you, Ontario Arts Council, for your financial support. Thank you, Second Story Press, for publishing great books by Canadian authors.

A big thank-you to editor Jordan for your invaluable guidance and insight into the story, your meticulous editing, and all the nitty gritty details that made the story shine. Thank you to the Sales and Marketing teams for ensuring this book gets into the hands of children.

Thank you, Lux. Always a little fearful of dogs, I became a dog lover when Lux came into our lives. And yes, one summer he did get lost in the Alberta wilderness when every evening there were thunderstorms and a lot of rain. Animal Services advised us to call off the search, but we could not and did not give up. What an unbelievably joyous moment when we found Lux, our miracle dog.

Finally, lots of love and gratitude to my husband, Mahmoud, for reading my messy draft, and to my children, Astrum and Shaira, and my son-in-law Sameer, for their support and cheering me on.

ABOUT THE AUTHOR

SHENAAZ NANJI is an internationally published author of over a dozen books for children. She holds an MFA in Writing from Vermont College. Her novel, *Child of Dandelions*, was a finalist for the Governor General's Award in Children's Literature. Her chapter book, *Alina in a Pinch*, was a finalist for the Silver Birch Express and the Hackmatack Children's Choice Book awards. Born in Kenya, she now lives in Calgary.